My dearest puppy, Storm

I hope this letter reaches you safe and sound. You have been so brave since you had to flee from the evil wolf Shadow.

Do not worry about me. I will hide here until you are strong enough to return and lead our pack. For now you must move on – you must hide from Shadow and his spies. If Shadow finds this letter I believe he will try to destroy it . . .

Find a good friend – someone to help finish my message to you. Because what I have to say to you is important. What I have to say is this: you must always

Please don't feel lonely. Trust in your friends and all will be well.

Your loving mother,

Canista

Sue Bentley's books for children often include animals, fairies and wildlife. She lives in Northampton and enjoys reading, going to the cinema, relaxing by her garden pond and watching the birds feeding their babies on the lawn. At school she was always getting told off for daydreaming or staring out of the window – but she now realizes that she was storing up ideas for when she became a writer. She has met and owned many cats and dogs and each one has brought a special kind of magic to her life.

Sue Bentley

School of Mischief

Illustrated by Angela Swan

PUFFIN

To Reuben – a boisterous and bouncy

spotty boy

PUFFIN BOOKS

Published by the Penguin Group
Penguin Books Ltd, 80 Strand, London WC2R 0RL, England
Penguin Group (USA) Inc., 375 Hudson Street, New York, New York 10014, USA
Penguin Group (Canada), 90 Eglinton Avenue East, Suite 700, Toronto, Ontario, Canada M4P 2Y3
(a division of Pearson Penguin Canada Inc.)
Penguin Ireland, 25 St Stephen's Green, Dublin 2, Ireland (a division of Penguin Books Ltd)
Penguin Group (Australia), 250 Camberwell Road, Camberwell, Victoria 3124, Australia
(a division of Pearson Australia Group Pty Ltd)
Penguin Books India Pvt Ltd, 11 Community Centre, Panchsheel Park, New Delhi – 110 017, India
Penguin Group (NZ), 67 Apollo Drive, Rosedale, North Shore 0632, New Zealand
(a division of Pearson New Zealand Ltd)
Penguin Books (South Africa) (Pty) Ltd, 24 Sturdee Avenue, Rosebank,
Johannesburg 2196, South Africa

Penguin Books Ltd, Registered Offices: 80 Strand, London WC2R 0RL, England

puffinbooks.com

First published 2008

013

Text copyright © Sue Bentley, 2008
Illustrations copyright © Angela Swan, 2008
All rights reserved

The moral right of the author and illustrator has been asserted

Set in Bembo
Typeset by Palimpsest Book Production Limited,
Grangemouth, Stirlingshire
Printed and bound in Great Britain by Clays Ltd, Elcograf S.p.A.

British Library Cataloguing in Publication Data
A CIP catalogue record for this book is available from the British Library

ISBN: 978–0–141–32382–4

www.greenpenguin.co.uk

MIX
Paper from
responsible sources
FSC   FSC® C018179
www.fsc.org

Penguin Books is committed to a sustainable
future for our business, our readers and our planet.
This book is made from Forest Stewardship
Council™ certified paper.

Prologue

Storm padded silently across the frozen lake. The young silver-grey wolf took a deep breath of the cold air. It felt good to be back.

Suddenly, a terrifying howl rang out, echoing in the violet night sky.

'Shadow!' gasped Storm. The powerful lone wolf who had attacked the Moon-claw pack was very close.

Storm should have known that it wasn't safe to return.

There was a bright flash of light and a dazzling burst of golden sparks. Where the young wolf had been standing there was now a tiny puppy with fluffy grey-and-white-fur, a round face and midnight-blue eyes.

Storm hoped this disguise would protect him until he found a place to hide.

Over by the shore, thick clumps of rushes stuck up through the ice. Storm sped towards them, his little furry sides heaving. On reaching the rushes, he flattened his belly against the ice and crawled into them.

There was a crackling of broken stems nearby. A dark mass appeared and a large paw, almost as big as Storm was now, reached out and scooped him up.

Storm whimpered with terror. His claws scrabbled desperately as he was drawn backwards.

'Be calm, my son,' growled a deep gentle voice. 'You are safe for the moment.'

'Mother!' Storm yipped with relief. His whole body wriggled and his grey-and-white tail twirled as he licked Canista's muzzle.

Canista's gold eyes softened as she smiled down at her tiny disguised cub. 'I am glad to see you again, but you cannot stay. Shadow is looking for you. He wants to lead the Moon-claw pack.'

Storm's lip curled, exposing needle-sharp puppy teeth. 'Is it not enough that

3

he killed my father and litter brothers
and wounded you? We must fight
Shadow and make him leave our lands!'

Canista shook her large head. 'He is
too strong for you and I am still weak
from his poisoned bite and cannot help
you,' she rumbled gently. 'The others
will not follow Shadow while you live.
Go back to the other world. Return
when you are wiser and stronger . . .'
She bit back a wince of pain.

Storm hated to leave her, but he
knew his mother was right. Opening
his mouth, he huffed out a glittering
puppy breath. The sparkly golden mist
whirled round Canista's injured paw
and then sank into her grey fur.

'Thank you, Storm. I feel a little
stronger,' she breathed.

Another fierce howl rang out and there came the sound of mighty paws thundering across the ice.

'Go now! Save yourself, Storm!' urged Canista.

Storm whimpered as he felt the power building inside him. Bright gold sparks ignited in his fluffy grey-and-white fur. A bright light glowed around him. And grew brighter . . .

Chapter
ONE

Freya Harding sat on the rug in her gran's smart flat. Sunlight poured in on to the Victorian doll's house that stood open in front of her.

Usually, Freya loved playing with all the miniature dolls and furniture, but even that couldn't cheer her up today. She sighed as she tucked a strand of brown hair behind one ear.

'Are you all right, pet?' asked Granny Harding, looking up from her newspaper where she was doing sudoku puzzles.

'I was just wondering if my old friends were missing me yet,' Freya said wistfully. It was right at the beginning of the school summer holidays and she and her parents had moved to Piddington to be closer to Granny Harding.

Gran put down the newspaper and took off her glasses. 'A lovely girl like you! Of course they are,' she said, smiling. 'I expect they'll keep in touch. But you're bound to make lots of new friends when you start your new school.'

'That won't be for ages,' Freya grumbled.

'Time passes more quickly when you're having fun,' said Gran. 'Do you fancy doing some cooking? We could pretend we're a couple of TV chefs!'

'I don't really feel like it. Couldn't I go back to the new house? I'll play computer games or email my old friends until Mum gets back.'

Gran shook her head. 'I'm afraid not, love. We agreed that you'd stay here with me while your parents are at work.'

Freya's shoulders slumped. 'I am nine years old. I know heaps of kids my age who look after themselves for the whole day.'

'Well, you're not going to be one of them,' Gran said firmly. 'If you're feeling restless you can pop out to the shop.' She stood up and reached for her

handbag. 'Here's some money. Will you get a loaf and some milk, please? And buy yourself a comic.'

'Gra-an! No one says, "comic" any more!' Freya teased.

Gran's eyes sparkled. 'Get a mag, then. Same difference, you cheeky baggage! But if you're not that bothered . . .'

'No, I'll go,' Freya said hurriedly. It was something to do and the village store was interesting in a weird kind of way. It sold boring stuff like knitting wool and dusty little cards of pins, but it also had yummy old-fashioned sweets in big glass jars.

Freya opened the flat door. 'I'll bring you a treat back. Lemon sherbets or pear drops?' she called over her shoulder.

'Surprise me!' Gran called.

Freya went downstairs and out of the converted shoe factory building. The shop was just down the street. As she opened the door a bell clanged loudly. A man popped his head out of a back room. 'I won't be a minute. Give me a shout when you've got what you came for,' he called.

'OK, fine,' Freya replied, but he'd disappeared again.

Freya looked around at the cluttered shelves of the quiet little shop. There didn't seem to be anyone to talk to or to make friends with in this new village. Freya sighed as she realized she was just going to have to make do with Gran's company for the summer until her new school began.

She wandered over to the big glass
jars of sweets to choose something her
gran might like, when she was stopped
in her path by a bright golden flash
that lit up the whole shop.

Freya rubbed her eyes, blinded for a
minute. One of the shop's display lights
must have been faulty.

When she could finally see again,
Freya opened her eyes to see a realistic-
looking toy sheepdog puppy. It was

sitting on the shelf right in front of her, squeezed in among the glass jars. The toy was very lifelike, with fluffy grey-and-white fur and sparkling midnight-blue eyes, peeping out from beneath a fuzzy little fringe.

'Oh, aren't you gorgeous! I wonder how much you are?' she said.

'I am not for sale!' the puppy woofed. 'Can you help me, please?'

Chapter
TWO

'Wow!' Freya blinked in fascination. The cute toy puppy must have some sort of noise-activated computer chip inside. 'Say something else!'

Freya leaned towards it. 'Grr-uf! Grr-uf!' she said, hoping that the sound of her voice would make it speak again.

The puppy blinked and stood up, balancing carefully on the shelf. Its little

tail drooped and just the end of it
started wagging. 'I am afraid that I do
not understand you. I am Storm of the
Moon-claw pack. What is your name?'

Freya's jaw dropped and she did a
double take. 'You . . . you're . . . real!'

Storm nodded. 'Yes, I am.' He put his
little head on one side and looked at
her with big serious midnight-blue eyes.

Freya swallowed, not quite sure that
this was really happening. She looked
up at the shop counter to see if the

shopkeeper was watching, but he still
hadn't returned from the storeroom.

Freya realized that the little puppy
seemed to be waiting for her to reply.
'I . . . I'm Freya. Freya Harding,' she
found herself gulping.

Storm dipped his fluffy little head.
'I am honoured to meet you, Freya,'
he yapped politely.

Freya was still puzzled. 'Um . . .
thanks. But how come you can talk?
And where did you come from?'

'All of my kind can talk. I have come
from another world, which is far away.
I need to hide from the fierce lone
wolf who attacked us — he is called
Shadow,' the tiny puppy told her. His
furry little brow wrinkled in a frown.
'Shadow wants to lead the Moon-claw

16

pack. I am the only cub left. The other wolves are waiting for me to grow strong and become their leader.'

Freya frowned, confused. 'Wolves? Cub? But you're just a tiny pup—'

Storm lifted his chin. 'Stand back, please. I will show you!'

There was another dazzling burst of golden light and a fountain of bright sparks sprayed out and sizzled as they trickled down all around Freya.

The tiny cute puppy had disappeared from the shelf. Standing in the aisle before her was an impressive young silver-grey wolf with glowing midnight-blue eyes and a thick neck-ruff that seemed to glitter with a thousand tiny gold diamonds.

'Storm?' Freya gasped, backing away

as she eyed the young wolf's muscular body, huge paws and big sharp teeth.

'Yes, it is still me, Freya. Do not be afraid. I will not harm you,' Storm said in a deep velvety growl.

And then, before Freya had time to get used to seeing Storm as his majestic real self, there was a final blinding flash

of light and Storm appeared once more as a tiny helpless grey-and-white puppy.

Freya blinked hard. 'Wow! That's so cool. What a brilliant disguise!'

Storm looked up at her from the floor and she noticed that he was beginning to tremble all over. 'My disguise will not fool Shadow. He is looking for me. I need to hide now.'

Freya bent down and reached out her hand. Storm sidled up close. He sniffed her hand and then licked her fingers with his warm pink tongue. Freya's soft heart went out to the scared little pup. Storm was amazing as his real self, but as a tiny helpless puppy with fuzzy grey-and-white fur, a long fringe and the brightest midnight-blue eyes she had ever seen, he was totally irresistible.

19

'I'm taking you back to my gran. She'll know what to do. Just wait until I tell her all about you,' she decided, picking him up.

'No!' Storm woofed. He twisted round to look up into her face. 'No one must know my secret. You must promise never to tell anyone, Freya!'

'OK,' Freya said quickly, to reassure him. She really wished she could have told Gran, who was great at keeping secrets, but if it meant her magical new friend would be safe, she was prepared to agree. 'I'll just say that you're a stray or something.'

Storm nodded. 'Thank you, Freya.'

The shopkeeper came out of the back room with a box in his arms and put it on the counter. 'Hello there. Did you

find what you wanted?' he called.

'Oh . . . er . . . yes, thanks. Just coming,' Freya said, quickly putting Storm down. 'Maybe you'd better hide and then you can slip outside with me when I leave,' she whispered to Storm.

Storm nodded. 'That is a good plan.' He quickly scampered under a rack of postcards.

Freya grabbed a loaf of bread and a

plastic container of milk from the fridge. As she went to pay for them her thoughts were racing.

A few moments ago, she'd been lonely and fed up and wondering how she was going to get through the next few weeks. Now she had the most marvellous new puppy friend anyone could wish for!

Chapter
THREE

'Oh my goodness!' said Gran as Freya
came into the sitting room with Storm
in her arms. 'Wherever did you get that
puppy?'

'I . . . um . . . found him outside the
shop. He was all by himself. I'm sure he's
a stray, so I've told him . . . I . . . um . . .
mean I've decided to look after him,'
Freya said, quickly correcting herself.

'Now don't go getting carried away, pet,' Gran said in a sensible tone. 'I expect his owner's nearby. That puppy looks like he's been well cared for.'

'But Storm was definitely by himself. I had a really good scout round. There was no one looking for a puppy,' Freya said. 'And there's no card in the shop window about a lost pup.'

Gran nodded thoughtfully. 'Well, he's not wearing a collar. Perhaps he might be a stray after all.' She reached out to stroke Storm's fuzzy little head. 'Storm, eh? It suits him. Isn't he gorgeous. He looks like an Old English sheepdog puppy to me. But as for keeping him . . . Well, I don't expect your mum and dad will be at all keen.'

Freya's heart sank as she realized Gran

was right. She'd wanted a pet for ages
but hadn't been allowed to have one
because no one was at home for most
of the day. But Freya had promised to
help Storm and she wasn't going to
give up that easily.

'It's not fair,' she said glumly. 'I always
have to do what Mum and Dad want.
No one ever lets *me* do *anything*!'

She stomped across the room and

plonked herself down on to the sofa.
Storm trotted after her and she picked
him up and settled him on her lap.

Storm yawned. 'I am very tired. I will
sleep now,' he yapped. Tucking his little
button-black nose under his soft front
paws, he closed his eyes.

Freya tensed, amazed that Storm had
just spoken, but Gran didn't appear to
have noticed anything odd. She stood
there, tapping her chin thoughtfully.

Freya leaned over and kissed the top
of Storm's fluffy head. 'Be careful. Gran
almost heard you,' she warned him in a
whisper.

'Only you can hear me talk, Freya.
Everyone else will think I'm barking,'
Storm woofed sleepily.

Freya sat up again. That was so cool!

Gran checked her watch. 'Your mum will be here to pick you up in an hour. I'll have a word with her about Storm. Maybe we can work something out.'

'Really?' Freya said excitedly. 'Thanks, Gran.'

'Now don't you go getting your hopes up. I'm not promising anything,' said Gran, reaching for the bag of shopping and peering inside. Her eyes twinkled. 'Although, those lemon sherbets might have helped.'

'Oops.' Freya gave a sheepish grin. After finding Storm it was a total miracle she'd remembered anything from the shop!

Freya held her breath and crossed her fingers and toes as her mum sat with a cup of tea on her lap. *Please, please, please, let her agree to me keeping Storm,* she thought.

'. . . and I wouldn't mind having Storm here in the daytime, when school term starts. I miss dear old Snowdrop. And I could do with a bit of dog-walking exercise,' Gran was saying.

Snowdrop was Gran's beloved miniature poodle, who had died over a year ago.

Mrs Harding sipped her tea. She wore her smart dark-green work suit and a white blouse. 'I hadn't banked on having a puppy, but I suppose Storm would be company for Freya during the holidays,' she mused. 'If you'll have him when we're not at home, Mum, it might work out.'

'So we can keep Storm?' Freya burst out, unable to keep quiet any longer.

Her mum smiled. 'On one condition. Storm goes to the vet for a health check-up and if someone claims him as their lost puppy, we hand him over – no arguments.'

'Fine!' Freya was prepared to agree to anything. She gently scooted the sleepy

puppy over on to the sofa cushion and then went and threw her arms round her gran and her mum in turn.

'Yay! That's *so* brilliant. Thanks, Mum. Thanks, Gran. You're the best!'

'We'd better be off,' Mrs Harding said. 'I need to pop to the shops to get something for supper. We can get some dog food and other bits too while we're there. Can you carry Storm out to the car?'

'Sure thing! Come on, sleepy-head! We're going home,' Freya whispered as she gently scooped Storm into her arms.

Storm stretched, pushing against her T-shirt with stiffened front legs and then he leaned up to lick her chin. 'Thank you, Freya,' he woofed gratefully.

Mrs Harding wrinkled her nose. 'Don't let him do that, dear. And I don't want Storm in your bedroom until the vet's checked him over. He's probably riddled with worms and all sorts.'

Storm sat bolt upright. 'I do not have worms!' he yapped indignantly.

It was all Freya could do not to burst out laughing at the look on his little grey-and-white round face.

Chapter
FOUR

The following day Freya woke early, too excited to sleep any longer. She was about to fling herself out of bed and dash straight down to the conservatory, where her mum had insisted Storm slept.

But something warm and furry was curled up in the crook of her arm. 'Good morning,' woofed a bright little voice.

'Storm?' Freya exclaimed. 'How did you get up here? Mum will go spare if she comes in and finds you on the bed!' She turned over to cuddle Storm and began stroking his fluffy grey-and-white fur.

Storm gave her a cheeky doggy grin. 'I have used my magic so that only you can see me.'

'Wow! You can make yourself invisible too?' Freya said. Storm was just full of surprises. She wondered what else her magical little friend could do.

Later on that morning, Freya stood outside her gran's, waving as her mum pulled away from the kerb. 'See you this evening!' she called.

While her mum was at work, Gran was taking Freya and Storm to the pet care centre to get Storm checked out by the vet. After that he could officially sleep in Freya's room.

Gran had sorted out a small pet carrier. 'It used to be Snowdrop's. It should be just the right size for Storm.'

Freya nodded. 'Good idea.'

As Gran was fetching her jacket, Storm eyed the carrier warily. 'I do not think I want to go into a cage,' he barked.

'People usually take their dogs to the vet in a carrier. You won't have to be in it for long,' Freya explained.

'Very well,' Storm woofed. He still didn't look too happy, but he allowed Freya to lift him into the carrier and fasten the door.

It was only a short walk to the pet care centre. The waiting room was filled with a variety of people and their pets. While Gran gave their details to the receptionist, Freya sat on a chair with the pet carrier on her knees.

A boy of about her own age was sitting opposite. He had a shock of floppy dark hair. His little black mongrel puppy kept weaving in and

out of his owner's legs, getting his lead
in a dreadful tangle.

Freya grinned. 'He looks like a
handful,' she said to the boy.

The boy shook his head. 'Tell me
about it!' He frowned at the little dog.
'Teddy. Sit!' he ordered, but the puppy
ignored him and dived under his chair.

'Freya Harding?' called a nurse from
one of the treatment rooms.

'That was quick.' Freya smiled at the
boy and his puppy on her way past. She
placed the carrier with Storm in it on
the examination table. Gran followed
her in.

The vet smiled at Freya. She wore a
white coat and had short black hair,
smooth dark skin and twinkly eyes.
'What can we do for you, young lady?'

'Mum says Storm has to have a check-up. We've only just got him,' Freya said. 'He's a stray, but I'm sure there's nothing wrong with him.'

The vet nodded. 'You're probably right, but it's sensible to make sure with a new puppy.' She opened the carrier and lifted Storm out. 'Hello, Storm. You're lovely, aren't you?'

Storm allowed the vet to check his
eyes and teeth and part his fur to
look for fleas. He even let her roll him
on to his back and pat his round little
tummy.

'Well, he's a fine healthy pup with no
obvious problems,' the vet said. 'He's
about the right age for his first
vaccination. As he's a stray, I don't
expect he'll have had it. I could do that
now, if you like?'

'Um . . . I'm not sure.' Freya stiffened.
She hadn't expected this.

'What is a vaccination?' Storm
woofed.

Freya quickly checked that Gran was
speaking to the nurse and the vet was
busy tapping Storm's details into a
nearby computer. 'It's an injection to

stop you getting diseases. Is that OK?'
she whispered.

'Injection?' Storm frowned in
puzzlement.

Freya didn't expect that any of the
magical wolves in the Moon-claw
pack had ever visited a vet. Before she
could elaborate, the vet reached up to a
shelf and turned back to the table. She
was holding a syringe with a long
needle.

Storm's eyes widened in alarm. He
stiffened and laid back his ears. 'I do
not need this medicine! My magic
protects me,' he barked.

'Hold him still, please. He's bound to
wriggle a bit,' the vet said. The nurse
grabbed Storm and held him firmly.

'No, wait! Don't give him it!' Freya

cried. 'He said that . . . I mean, I don't think . . .'

'It's all right, love. I hated it when Snowdrop had injections too,' Gran interrupted gently. 'The vet won't hurt Storm. She knows what she's doing.'

No, she doesn't, Freya thought desperately. *Storm's not like any puppy she has ever treated! He's not even from this world!*

But there was no way she could

explain without giving away Storm's secret and anyway, she doubted if anyone would believe her.

Suddenly, Freya felt a strange warm tingling sensation down her spine as miniature gold sparks twinkled deep within Storm's fuzzy grey-and-white fur.

Something very strange was about to happen.

Chapter
FIVE

To Freya's complete amazement the vet
and nurse jerked their hands away from
Storm as if they'd both been stung. In a
stream of golden sparkles that only
Freya could see, they shot backwards
across the room, as if they were on
roller skates.

Gran took a step back in surprise as
Storm did a giant leap off the

examination table and landed on
the floor, on all fours, right beside
the door.

'Let me out!' he yelped.

As Freya moved towards him, another
nurse popped her head into the room.
Storm saw his chance. He dodged
round her and shot into the waiting
room.

The vet and the nurse stood there
with stunned expressions. They began
blinking and rubbing their eyes as if
they were coming out of some kind of
trance.

'Storm's just . . . a bit nervous. We'll
. . . um . . . make another appointment
when he's calmed down,' Freya burbled.
'Bye! I have to catch him!'

Freya rushed out and sprinted across

the waiting room. The receptionist, the boy with the little black mongrel and the other pet owners gaped at her, but Freya ignored them all.

Storm was pawing frantically at the front door. 'It's all right. I'm here,' she crooned, picking him up and taking him outside. 'I'm sorry you were so scared. The vet didn't understand that you aren't a normal puppy and I could hardly explain, could I?'

Storm blinked up at her from under his fringe. 'You did your best, Freya. Do not worry. I am fine now!'

Freya breathed a sigh of relief. 'I'm glad you could use your magic without giving yourself away.'

Gran emerged from the waiting room with the empty pet carrier. 'Oh, thank

heavens. You've caught him! I've never seen a dog jump like that before. Maybe we should change Storm's name to Skippy!'

'Who?' Freya asked, puzzled.

'Skippy. He was a kangaroo in an old TV series,' Gran explained. 'Anyway, I had a quick word with the vet. She says we can bring Storm back any time for his vaccination.'

'Um . . . right,' Freya murmured. She

guessed that there was no way anyone
would get Storm to go back there now,
but she didn't say so.

'In the meantime, the vet did say Storm
was healthy, so that should satisfy your
mum,' Gran reasoned. 'Why don't you
take Storm for a walk now to calm him
down. There's a park just round the
corner. I'll just pop this pet carrier back
to my flat and meet you there in a few
minutes.'

'OK. Thanks, Gran.' Freya was relieved
– she wasn't sure that Storm would be
able to magic himself out of trouble at
the vet's a second time!

They walked back with Gran to the
old shoe factory building, but then
carried on towards the park. As soon
as they came to the wrought-iron

park gates, Storm gave a happy woof
and ran inside.

Freya smiled as she watched the
tiny puppy rooting about in the grass
and searching for interesting smells.
Storm picked up a twig and came
lolloping towards her with it in his
mouth. As Freya strolled along, Storm
pranced beside her, proudly holding the
twig.

Some way ahead, Freya noticed the
same dark-haired boy with the small
black dog from the vet's. The little dog
was on a lead.

'It's the boy from the waiting room
and that's his naughty puppy, Teddy,'
Freya told Storm. 'Shall we go and say
hello?' Freya hadn't had a friend who
was a boy back at her old school, but

this boy had seemed friendly and it
would be nice to know someone her
own age in this village.

Storm nodded and dropped his twig,
wagging his tail eagerly.

The boy looked up and smiled as
they approached. 'Hi. Didn't I just see
you at the vet's? I'm Isaac.'

Freya smiled back. 'I'm Freya and this
is Storm.'

'Hi, Storm,' Isaac said, bending down
to stroke Storm. 'He's a gorgeous puppy.
What happened back there? I saw
Storm dash out of the examination
room and then you shot after him!'

'Oh, that. It was . . . er . . . just a
mix-up. It's sorted out now,' Freya said
vaguely, hoping to avoid more awkward
questions. She quickly changed the

subject. 'Teddy's really cute too. Have you had him long?' she asked.

Isaac glanced down at his shaggy little mongrel puppy. Teddy was still engrossed in sniffing something in the grass and seemed in a world of his own.

'Just a few weeks,' Isaac said. He pulled a face. 'It's a bit of a sore point.'

Freya was about to ask what he meant, but just then, Storm brushed against Teddy, his stumpy tail wagging as he barked a greeting.

Teddy's head whipped round in surprise. He launched himself at Storm and yanked the lead right out of Isaac's hand.

It happened so fast that Freya, Storm and Isaac were taken completely by surprise.

'Yipe!' Storm yelped as Teddy boisterously nipped his ear.

'Bad dog! Come here!' Isaac yelled at Teddy.

Still growling playfully, the little mongrel bounced down on to his front legs. Teddy eyed Storm warily, but seemed a bit calmer now that he'd checked Storm out.

'I said come here!' Isaac roared, but his puppy ignored him.

Freya took matters into her own hands. She stepped boldly between the two puppies and clapped her hands loudly. Storm jumped sideways in surprise, but Teddy just looked up at Freya to see who was standing in his way.

'That's enough!' she scolded, frowning

angrily and shaking one finger at the
little mongrel.

Teddy rushed towards his owner with
his tail between his legs. Isaac
immediately grabbed the trailing lead
and pulled Teddy to heel.

'Oh gosh. I'm sorry! I hope Storm
isn't hurt,' he said, scarlet with
embarrassment.

'Of course he is. Your dog just bit
him!' Freya snapped, too shaken up and
worried about Storm to be polite.

'Can't you control Teddy? Come here, Storm. Let me check your ear.'

Storm padded over and sat down obediently. 'Do not worry. It is not serious,' he woofed.

Freya examined his ear. There was a tiny cut where one of Teddy's teeth had caught it. 'It's bleeding a little bit,' she told Isaac. 'I'll have to take Storm back to my gran's flat and get his ear cleaned up. She lives in the factory flats.'

'I'll walk along with you – it's the least I can do,' Isaac said in a subdued voice. 'I live at the Gatehouse in Fern Avenue. It's just opposite the old shoe factory building.'

Freya picked Storm up as they set off, just in case Teddy felt like leaping on him again. But although the little mongrel strained at his lead and kept looking up at Storm, his tongue was lolling out in a friendly grin.

Freya was puzzled. Teddy seemed like a completely different dog now. They all walked through the park gates in silence and emerged on to the street.

Isaac chewed his lip and looked miserable. 'I'm really sorry,' he apologized again. 'I try to get Teddy to behave, but I'm rubbish at it. Dad reckons he's just too strong-willed for me. Yesterday, Teddy chewed a corner of our new rug. Mum nearly had kittens. And now this. Please don't tell anyone what just happened.'

Isaac looked genuinely upset and Freya felt her anger starting to drain away. 'Well, OK. I wouldn't want to get you into any more trouble,' she agreed.

'Aw, thanks,' Isaac said, relieved. He dropped to his knees in front of Teddy and took the puppy's little face in both hands. 'You're one shaggy little ball of trouble, aren't you?'

Teddy wagged his tail and licked Isaac's chin.

Freya's heart softened. There was no doubt that Isaac loved his little mongrel puppy.

'Why can't you ever behave yourself? You're never going to be let out of your cage,' Isaac said sadly to Teddy.

Cage? Freya didn't believe what she had just heard. She was too stunned to react.

But Storm wasn't. His head came up

and a tiny growl rumbled in his throat.
'That is not right. Dogs do not live in
cages!'

Freya's mind whirled. No wonder
Teddy was so badly behaved if he was
kept shut up. Any dog would have lots
of pent-up energy to get rid of.

'Yoo hoo!' called a familiar voice.

Freya saw Gran coming down the street
towards them. She waved to her. 'That's
my Granny Harding,' she said to Isaac.

'Sorry I was held up, pet,' Gran said
as she reached them. 'A friend just
phoned me and I had a job getting
away.' She smiled at Isaac. 'You're the
boy from the vet's, aren't you? I'm glad
to see that Freya's made a new friend.
Maybe you'd all like to come back and
have tea –'

'Gran,' Freya interrupted quickly. 'Storm's hurt his ear. We have to clean it and put some cream on it.'

'Oh dear. How did that happen?' Gran said, frowning.

'It was an accident. He caught it on something in the grass,' Freya fibbed.

Isaac shot her a grateful look.

Gran bent down to look at Storm's ear. 'It must have only been a scratch. It's already drying up,' she said as she stood up. She smiled at Freya and Isaac. 'Well, shall we go, you two?'

Isaac looked uncomfortable. 'Thanks very much for the invitation, Mrs Harding. But I . . . er . . . have to get home. Maybe some other time? I'll see you around, Freya,' he said, edging away.

'Bye,' Freya said, watching Isaac cross

the road and head for Fern Avenue,
with Teddy straining at his lead.

'He seems like a nice lad,' Gran
commented.

Freya didn't answer. Isaac had seemed
really nice. She had started wondering if
they might become friends, but now
she was confused. There was no way
she could ever like a boy who allowed
his puppy to be kept in a cage.

Chapter
SIX

Two mornings later, Freya was busy
in the kitchen making breakfast as
a Saturday treat for her mum and
dad.

As the toast pinged up out of the
toaster, Freya sighed. She hadn't been
able to stop thinking about Teddy. Was
the little mongrel shut up in a small
cage right now?

'What are we going to do about Teddy?' she asked Storm.

Storm was sitting curled up on a chair, watching as Freya placed the breakfast things on a tray.

His bright midnight-blue eyes glinted. 'I have a plan! We will go and rescue him.'

'Really?' Freya said, doubtfully. 'How can we, without anyone noticing? And then what are we going to do with Teddy? Just let me take this lot up to Mum and Dad and then you can tell me what you have in mind. OK?'

Storm nodded.

As Freya folded the morning papers under one arm and went into the hall, she didn't see the mischievous look on the tiny puppy's face.

Upstairs, Freya knocked on her parents' bedroom door before going in. 'Here you go! I thought you'd like a lie-in,' she said.

Her mum sat up looking sleepy-eyed. 'Thanks, love. That's sweet of you.'

There was a grunt from beneath the mound of covers and her dad peeked out. His hair was all standing on end. 'You're a star, Freya.'

'I'm just going to take Storm out for a walk. See you later,' Freya told them.

'Don't go too far. And remember to keep him on his lead. You don't want him dashing into the road,' her mum cautioned.

Freya nodded, although she knew that her magical little friend would never do anything so dangerous. Storm was

already waiting by the front door when she padded downstairs.

Freya slipped Storm's new collar and lead into her shorts' pocket. 'I'd better take these. We're supposed to be pretending that you're an ordinary puppy –' She stopped suddenly, as she felt a now familiar warm prickling sensation run down her spine.

She saw bright gold sparks igniting in Storm's fluffy grey-and-white fur and the tips of his ears were crackling with electricity.

'What's going on?' she asked him, intrigued.

But Storm gave her a mysterious doggy grin. Lifting one fuzzy little paw, he sent a glittering burst of power towards her. A golden mist spun round Freya. She felt a sense of lightness flicker all through her body. There was a *whoosh* of movement and then she and Storm were flying straight *through* the front door and zooming upwards into the air together.

'Wow! This is brilliant!' Freya couldn't contain her excitement at what was happening. She held out her arms as they drifted along above the streets and houses. Storm's grey-and-white fur rippled in the breeze and Freya's hair streamed out behind her.

'Where are we going, Storm?'

'You will see very soon,' replied Storm mysteriously as his little puppy ears flapped in the wind.

They flew above treetops and almost brushed the top of a church spire. Freya spotted the old shoe factory and then they began drifting downwards towards a detached old-fashioned red-brick house.

Freya's feet touched grass as she landed beside Storm. They were in a back garden, with neat paths and flower beds.

An idea suddenly popped into Freya's head. 'Is this Isaac's house?'

Storm nodded enthusiastically. 'We are going to take Teddy to a new home!'

'Hang on a minute . . .' Freya began, not sure that Storm had really thought this through. But with another *whoosh* of gold sparks they were shooting through the house walls.

'Oof!' Freya breathed as they silently exploded into a large modern kitchen. It had lots of cupboards and stainless steel things. There was a smart table and chairs at one end.

Luckily, the kitchen was empty. Part of the floor was taken up by a roomy wire pen with a cosy bed inside and dishes for food and water. Dog toys were strewn about. Teddy was curled up on a fleecy blanket, his paws twitching as he slept.

Freya frowned. She had expected to find Teddy shut up in a small cage

inside a garden shed, but this pen
looked more like a really swish pet
hotel.

Just then, Freya heard footsteps
coming towards the kitchen. She and
Storm were going to be discovered at
any second!

'Quick, Storm. Do something!' Freya
whispered.

Just as the kitchen door began to
open, there was a tiny flash of gold

light and Freya felt herself tingling all over. There was a collapsing sensation and the table and chair legs seemed to shoot up around Freya like giant trees.

Storm had made them the size of mice!

Quick as winking, Freya and Storm scuttled behind a chair leg. They watched as a giant woman in a dressing gown, who Freya guessed was probably Isaac's mum, forked dog food into a bowl and opened the pen to put it inside. 'Here you go, boy,' she said.

Teddy's nose twitched as he smelled the food. He leapt out of bed, tail wagging, and started to chomp the food.

Isaac's mum bent down to watch him. 'I hope those new puppy-training

classes are going to work. Isaac really
wants to keep you and we do too. If
you weren't so destructive in the house,
you wouldn't have to sleep in your pen,
would you?' She sighed. 'I do hope we
don't have to find you a new home.
It'll break Isaac's heart.'

'She seems really nice, doesn't she?'
Freya whispered to Storm.

Storm nodded.

Freya felt a stir of guilt. 'We got it all
wrong, didn't we? Teddy might be a real
problem pup, but Isaac and his mum
and dad are being really good to him.'

'Teddy does not need to be rescued,'
Storm woofed in agreement, looking as
shame-faced as Freya.

Isaac's mum went and opened the
back door into the garden, before

returning to the kitchen and opening cupboards. Fresh air and sunlight poured into the room.

'Come on,' Freya urged, seeing their chance. She sped towards the back door on her tiny legs and scrambled down the step and into the garden. Storm ran alongside her.

Once outside they hurried along the path that led to the back gate and out of view of the kitchen. There was a faint stretching sensation and a noise like a squeaky balloon and Freya and Storm were normal size again.

'That was so cool!' Freya said, looking forward to flying home magically again. She stretched her arms out in a mock Supergirl pose. 'Let's go, Storm!'

But it was too late.

'Hey! What are you two doing here?' called a voice from above them.

Freya looked up to see Isaac peering down at them from his open bedroom window.

Chapter
SEVEN

'I didn't think I'd see you and Storm again so soon!' Isaac said, sounding pleased.

'Er . . . no,' Freya said, her mind racing. 'We came over to see if you and Teddy . . . um . . . wanted to meet up later or something,' she improvised.

Isaac grinned delightedly. 'Yeah, great idea. Maybe we could —' His face dropped as he seemed to remember something. 'Mum's arranged for me to take Teddy to training classes this afternoon. You wouldn't fancy coming to that, would you? It might be good for Storm too,' he said hopefully.

'I do not need training!' Storm yapped indignantly.

'Sounds like Storm's saying he'd love to come!' Isaac guessed.

Freya bit back a grin as Storm frowned and laid back his ears. 'Maybe we could just come and watch,' she said tactfully. 'Where's it being held?'

'The community centre, next to the church. It starts at 2 p.m.'

'I know where that is. OK, I'll check with my mum. If I'm coming, I'll see you there. Gotta go now,' Freya said as she remembered that her mum and dad would soon be wondering where she'd got to. She unbolted the garden gate, which opened directly into the side road.

'How come you two got in here, by the way?' Isaac asked, sounding puzzled.

Freya thought quickly. How was she going to explain the locked gate? 'I'm a good climber! Couldn't resist it,' she said, quickly slipping outside and closing the gate.

There was no one in sight and they couldn't be seen from Isaac's house. Across the road, a thick hedge screened the other houses. Once again Freya felt the light feeling spread through her as golden sparks swirled around and she and Storm zoomed up into the air.

They were back home in a trice. Her

mum was just walking down the stairs in her dressing gown, her hair still wet from the shower.

'Did you have a good walk?' Mrs Harding asked.

'Yes, thanks,' Freya said casually. She told her about bumping into Isaac and the dog-training classes. 'I said I might see Isaac there. Is that OK?'

'Of course it is. I'm going shopping later, so I can drop you and Storm off. We can meet up afterwards if you like and come home together.' Her mum smiled. 'I'm glad you're starting to make friends here.'

Freya smiled back, happy to know that Isaac looked after Teddy properly. 'Me too!'

★

'Put that puppy on a lead! At once, please!' A voice boomed as Freya walked into the training session with Storm in her arms. The instructor had her hair in a bun and wore a sleeveless, flowered dress and flat clumpy sandals.

Everyone turned round to look at Freya. Blushing, she placed Storm on the floor and clipped on his collar and lead. 'Sorry, Storm. Looks like they have strict rules here,' she whispered to him.

'I do not mind being captive for a short while,' Storm woofed amiably.

Freya spotted Isaac waving at them
from across the room. She and Storm
hurried over to him.

'Hi! I'm really glad you came!' Isaac
rolled his eyes. 'The instructor's a bit of
an old dragon, isn't she?'

Freya nodded. 'You can say that
again!'

There were about forty owners and
their dogs in the room. With people
talking and dogs barking, the noise was
deafening.

Storm's ears swivelled and he looked
up at Freya in concern.

'I expect it'll be quieter once the class
starts,' Freya said, patting him
reassuringly. She noticed that Teddy
didn't seem fazed by the noise. He was
wagging his tail and pulling at his lead

as if he wanted to play with the other
dogs.

'Get into a large circle, everyone.
Come along,' the instructor ordered,
waggling her hand at anyone who hung
back. 'That's it, don't be shy.'

Freya didn't dare say that she'd only
come to watch. This was the scariest
woman she'd ever met. She walked
forward and joined the circle. 'Come
on, Storm. Let's join in. It might be
fun,' she whispered.

Storm looked doubtful, but he trotted
after Freya nonetheless.

'I'm Lucy Jackman, but you can all
call me Lucy,' said the instructor.

The first exercise was teaching the
dogs to walk at heel. Two of Lucy's
helpers kept an eye on things and

offered words of advice if needed.

'Pull gently on the lead, while saying "Back" firmly, to bring your dog to heel,' one of them instructed.

Isaac tried, but Teddy kept dancing about and trying to bite his lead. He seemed more interested in all the other dogs and kept lunging at them, his tail wagging furiously.

Freya noticed that poor Isaac soon looked very hot and bothered.

'Next, we'll practise the recall,' Lucy said loudly. She explained how owners could teach their dogs to learn their names and to come when called.

Storm was enjoying himself and acting like an obedient pet, but Isaac was having great trouble with Teddy. The little mongrel wouldn't respond when his name was called, no matter how hard Isaac tried.

'It's hopeless,' Isaac groaned after another twenty minutes. 'Teddy's too boisterous. He's just not paying attention.'

'Well, it is only his first training session,' Freya commented.

'Yeah, I guess you're right,' Isaac said, shrugging.

'I'm going to demonstrate the basic

sit and stay now,' Lucy said. She walked over to Freya and held out her hand. 'May I borrow your puppy?'

'Um . . .' Freya couldn't think of a reason to refuse and she didn't think Lucy would have listened anyway. 'OK, then,' she murmured, handing over Storm's lead.

The trainer jerked on the lead so that Storm lifted his head and high-stepped into the centre of the room. Lucy suddenly stopped dead. 'Sit!' she ordered, pressing a firm hand on to Storm's hind-quarters. 'Be firm. Your puppy needs to know who's in charge,' she said briskly.

Storm blinked in surprise, but lowered his fuzzy bottom and sat down. Lucy smiled in a self-satisfied way. She put Storm's lead down and walked backwards slowly, saying, 'Stay!'

Storm did a doggy shrug. He yawned and scratched the fur on his tummy with one back leg and then got up and ambled over to Freya.

'I have had enough training now,' he yapped.

'OK. We'll sit this one out –' Freya began, reaching down to pat Storm, but before her fingers even brushed his fur, Lucy swooped forward and grabbed the little puppy's lead again.

As the trainer tried to drag him back into the middle of the room Storm gave a tiny growl of protest. He laid back his ears and straightened all four legs, so that his claws skittered across the wooden floor.

'Come along now. No naughty little pup's going to get the better of me!' Lucy said, with a determined glint in her eye.

Freya smiled inwardly. *Do you want to bet?* she thought.

Chapter
EIGHT

Storm threw back his head and
suddenly stopped dead.

Lucy was jerked to a halt so abruptly
that her clumpy sandals knocked
together with a loud clatter and she
almost fell over her own feet. The
trainer turned to Storm, her mouth
sagging open in surprise as she tried to
work out how a tiny puppy had

suddenly become as strong as a fully
grown Great Dane!

Sighing heavily, she picked Storm up
and tucked him firmly under one arm.
'This just won't do! Come along now.'

But the annoyed little puppy had a
rather unmagical solution to being
manhandled.

'Ugh!' Lucy cried as a sprinkle
dampened her flowery dress. 'He's wet
all over me!' She put Storm down

hastily, reached for a tissue and dabbed at her dress.

Storm scampered back to Freya and sat beside her, looking pleased with himself.

'Storm, you are *so* bad!' Freya scolded gently, her mouth twitching.

The rest of the class erupted with laughter, including Isaac. Most of the dogs began joining in, barking and yapping, all except Teddy who danced about on the spot.

'Good for you, Storm!' Isaac spluttered. 'That Lucy's such a bossyboots!'

Everyone grew calm and the class continued. The final exercise was retrieval. The puppies were supposed to pick something up and return with it

to their owners. Teddy simply grabbed
the rubber dumb-bell and ran round
the room with Isaac at his heels.

'I give up,' Isaac puffed, red-faced,
coming over to sit beside Freya and
Storm, who were sitting this one out.

The class ended ten minutes later and
the owners and their dogs all filed
outside. Freya stood talking to Isaac
before she went to meet her mum.
Storm and Teddy stood nose to nose,
their tails wagging companionably.

'Well, that was a lot of good. Not!'
Isaac said gloomily. 'Teddy was as
naughty and boisterous as he always is.'

'He'll be better next time. You'll see,'
Freya said encouragingly. 'Look, he
seems to be quite friendly with Storm
now.'

Isaac nodded, still looking downhearted. 'That's something, I suppose.'

Freya felt really sorry for him. Isaac tried so hard to get Teddy to behave. 'Do you fancy going for a walk across the fields tomorrow afternoon?' she said, hoping to cheer him up.

Isaac brightened up a bit. 'Yeah, OK. Do you want to meet outside your gran's flat after lunch? The field's quite near there.'

'See you there then! Bye for now.' Freya waved as she set off towards the shops to meet her mum.

Freya hadn't been asleep for long that night when she woke abruptly to the sound of growling and snapping. She blinked sleepily. She must be imagining it after having spent all day with naughty dogs.

But as the dogs continued to bark outside, Freya realized that she wasn't dreaming or imagining it. This was real.

Storm was tucked right under her chin, like a furry scarf, and Freya suddenly sensed that he was trembling

all over. As she sat up, Storm gave a mournful whine and ducked under the duvet.

'What's wrong?' Freya asked gently, lifting the duvet to look at him. 'Are you sick?'

'Shadow knows where I am! He has put a spell on those dogs outside, so that they will attack me,' Storm said in a muffled whimper.

Freya leapt out of bed and peered through a crack in the bedroom curtains. She could see a man standing under the street lamp struggling with two long-toothed dogs. Their pale eyes glinted in the moonlight.

As she watched, the man scolded the dogs and got them under control. Their scary faces seemed to soften. He led

them away and the growling and
snapping gradually faded.

Freya turned back to Storm. 'It's OK.
They've gone now. You're safe.' She got
back into bed and Storm crawled up
towards her. Freya gathered his warm
little body into her arms.

The tiny puppy was beginning to
calm down, but his big midnight-blue
eyes were wide and anxious. 'Shadow
will send more dogs to attack me.
Normal dogs will become just like
those you saw outside. I may have to
leave suddenly, without saying goodbye,'
he told Freya.

Freya felt a sharp pang. She couldn't
bear to think of losing her little friend.
'We could find somewhere else to hide
you, then maybe Shadow will give up

looking and you can stay with me
forever!'

Storm looked at her, his little round
face deadly serious. 'I cannot do that.
One day, I must return to my own
world to help my mother and lead the
other wolves. Do you understand that,
Freya?'

Freya nodded sadly, but she didn't
want to think about being so lonely
again. She felt determined to enjoy

every single second of her time spent with Storm. 'Let's go back to sleep,' she said, changing the subject. 'We're meeting Isaac and Teddy tomorrow. That's something to look forward to.'

Storm yawned and nodded. He cuddled into the crook of Freya's arm as she snuggled them both into a fold of the duvet.

Chapter
NINE

Isaac and Teddy were already waiting
outside the old shoe factory building
when Freya and Storm arrived the
following afternoon.

'Hi, Isaac. Hi, Teddy.' Freya bent down
to stroke the little dog's shaggy black
fur. Teddy bounced up and down madly,
whining and pawing at her. 'Too much
love! Calm down, boy,' Freya laughed.

Bending down she gently pushed the boisterous pup away.

Teddy sat down and looked at her quizzically.

'You seem to be able to get him to behave, but he takes no notice of me,' Isaac grumbled.

'I must have learned something from dog-training class after all. Even if Storm didn't!' Freya said.

She and Isaac laughed as they remembered what a disaster it had been.

'That Lucy woman was a nightmare, wasn't she? I hope it's a different trainer next time,' Isaac said as they started walking.

The field was only five minutes away, in the opposite direction to the park. Once there, Freya and Isaac let the puppies off their leads. Storm and Teddy immediately rushed around trying to sniff out rabbits.

Freya and Isaac walked along chatting and enjoying the warm sunshine. Bright yellow dandelions dotted the grass and pillowy clouds floated across the blue sky.

To one side of the field, Freya could see a big sign and a high wire fence round some partly built houses. The fence had been bashed down in one place. As it was a Sunday, there was no sign of any workers or heavy machinery.

Teddy suddenly spotted a rabbit that was heading for the gap in the fence. He flew after it and ran headlong on to the building site.

'Teddy! Come here! It's dangerous

over there!' Isaac called, breaking into a run.

Freya wasn't surprised when Teddy just kept on going. Storm ran up to her. 'Do not worry. I will go and fetch Teddy,' he panted.

Storm tore off ahead of them both as Freya ran to catch up with Isaac.

By the time Freya pounded up to the building site there was no sign of either puppy. Isaac was already standing there, looking around. 'Where are they?'

Freya shook her head. 'I don't know. I'll go this way. Why don't you look over there?'

'OK.' Isaac set off towards a big pile of sand.

Freya walked past a huge cement mixer, picking her way carefully over scattered bricks and bits of wood that were lying around. She glimpsed a small black shape scampering towards a plank that had been placed as a makeshift bridge over a deep ditch.

It was Teddy, and Storm was hot on his trail.

'Over here!' Freya yelled to Isaac, waving her arms.

Isaac appeared as Freya ran towards the ditch. She saw Teddy reach the plank bridge and scamper straight across. Storm bounded after him, but skidded on some mud.

With a yelp of alarm, he plunged into

the ditch. There was a splash as the tiny puppy fell into the muddy water at the bottom and sank out of sight.

'Storm!' Freya screamed as Storm's mud-covered little form rose into view again. Coughing, he began splashing about and searching for paw-holds in the sticky earth.

Isaac rushed up, his eyes wide with horror.

Freya realized that Storm probably couldn't use his magic without giving himself away. She didn't think twice. Thrusting the plank aside, she jumped into the ditch.

Mud splashed everywhere as Freya landed waist-high in the ditch. Her foot slid against a submerged brick and she gasped as pain shot up her ankle.

Ignoring it, she reached down and grabbed Storm. He scrabbled against her, his muddy fur plastering her T-shirt.

'Thank you for saving me,' he woofed, mud dripping from his muzzle.

'No problem,' Freya said, using a clean bit of T-shirt to wipe mud from his eyes and nose. 'I'm just glad you aren't hurt.'

'Are you two OK?' Isaac asked worriedly.

'Kind of,' Freya said, wincing at the sharp pain in her ankle. Now that Storm was safe, she was starting to feel sick and shaky.

'You are hurt. I will help you,' Storm yapped.

'But Isaac . . .' Freya stopped halfway through protesting as she felt a warm tingling sensation in her hands and golden sparks fizzed in Storm's fur, hidden beneath the thick coating of mud.

The pain in her ankle grew warmer and then icy cold and seemed to drain away completely, just as if she'd emptied out a packet of sugar. 'Thanks, Storm. I'm fine now,' she whispered.

'Can you climb out by yourself if you give Storm to me?' Isaac said, reaching down.

Freya nodded. She handed Storm up to him.

'All right, little fella? That must have been a nasty shock,' he crooned.

Freya scrambled out of the ditch and rose to her feet. Teddy came running towards them, his tongue lolling happily. His black fur was covered with sand and brick dust.

Freya quickly grabbed the little mongrel. 'Got you!' Isaac passed her Teddy's lead and Freya clipped it on to his collar. 'Oh heck. Look at the state of these two!' she said, looking down at the pair of messy pups.

'Have you seen yourself?' Isaac said.

'You look like you've had a bath in melted chocolate. And look at my T-shirt. Mum'll go spare if I arrive home like this.'

Freya nodded. 'Mine will too. What are we going to – Hang on, I've got an idea! Follow me!'

Chapter
TEN

'Hi, Gran!' Freya said ten minutes later,
as the flat door opened. 'Surprise!'

'Oh, my giddy aunt! What on earth
happened to you?' Granny Harding's
eyes widened in shock as she saw
the mess they were in. 'Right. Wait
there. I'll get some old newspapers.
You'd better take off your shoes
and then you can carry those pups

straight through to the bathroom.'

Freya flashed Isaac a grin as they
padded through the flat with their arms
full of muddy puppies. 'Gran always
knows what to do and she doesn't
make a mega-fuss like most grown-ups!'

An hour later, Storm and Teddy had
been bathed and Freya and Isaac's
clothes were whizzing round in Gran's
washer-drier. They sat there wearing
borrowed bathrobes, taking it in turns
to dry Teddy and Storm with the
hairdryer.

Storm wasn't too keen on the noisy
hairdryer, but Teddy didn't seem to
mind it. He closed his eyes, enjoying
the way the warm air ruffled his scruffy
black fur.

'There. You're all done.' Freya stroked

Storm's cotton-wool-soft grey-and-
white fur. 'Mmm. You smell wonderful.'

Storm gave her an unimpressed look
from under an extremely fluffy thatch
of fringe.

Freya and Isaac erupted with laughter.
'Sorry, Storm. But you should see your
face,' she apologized in a whisper.

Gran came in from the kitchen and
put a plate of sandwiches, crisps and a
home-made chocolate cake on the table.
'I thought you might like these.'

'Thanks, Gran. You're the best!' Freya said.

'Yeah. Thanks loads, Mrs Harding,' Isaac said politely. 'And thanks for being so brilliant about this.'

Gran smiled. 'Don't mention it, pet. It's nice for me to have unexpected visitors.'

While Isaac finished drying Teddy, Gran produced a box of dog biscuits. She doled them out to the clean, dry puppies. Teddy and Storm lay on the rug, chomping away happily as Freya and Isaac went to sit at the table.

'Tuck in, you two,' Gran said, pouring cups of tea. 'Oh, I've forgotten the knife and cake forks. Could you get them for me, Freya? They're on a tray in the kitchen.'

Freya went into the kitchen and returned with the tray. Just as she was approaching the table, Teddy jumped up, pawing at her legs. 'Oh!' Freya stumbled as she tried to avoid stepping on him. The tray of cutlery flew out of her hands. It fell to the ground with an almighty crash, right beside Teddy.

Gran and Isaac almost jumped out of their skins.

'Yike!' Storm screeched in shock, leaping to his feet with his fur all standing on end.

But Teddy was still nosing around for biscuit crumbs and didn't seem upset at all.

'That's odd,' Freya said.

'What is, love?' asked Gran.

'Well,' Freya began. 'Teddy didn't react

at all to the loud noise right next to
him. It's just as if he didn't hear it . . .'
A suspicion jumped into her mind.
'Isaac, can you stroke Teddy to distract
him for a minute?'

Isaac looked puzzled, but he tickled
Teddy's chest. Teddy wagged his tail and
nibbled Isaac's fingers.

Freya went and stood behind them.
She clapped her hands loudly. Teddy
didn't look round and his ears didn't
even flicker.

Freya looked across at Isaac. 'I think I
know why Teddy seems to be such a
problem. He's not naughty. He could
be deaf,' she said gently.

'Deaf?' Isaac echoed. 'But he can't be.
The vet looked in his ears when he
checked him over. He would have

noticed if something was wrong, wouldn't he?'

'Not necessarily,' said Gran. 'If Teddy was born that way, there might be no outward sign – it can be easy to miss in puppies. People assume that they don't learn their names or come when they're called because they're young and boisterous or just naughty.'

'Just like Teddy,' Isaac said wonderingly.

'Exactly!' Freya cast her mind back. 'It makes sense, when you think about it. Teddy probably turned on Storm in the park, because he couldn't hear him coming and thought he was being attacked. Teddy didn't react when I clapped my hands, but when he saw me frowning and wagging my finger at

him, he got the message! Do you
remember?'

Isaac nodded. 'He knew he'd done
wrong then, didn't he? And those other
times when he seemed to obey you,
you were actually looking at him, so he
understood what you wanted him to
do,' he recalled eagerly.

Freya nodded, feeling even more
certain that she was right about Teddy.

Isaac dropped down beside Teddy and hugged him. 'Poor little chap. It's not your fault. You can't help it, can you?'

Teddy licked Isaac's face and looked perfectly happy.

Freya took the opportunity to whisper to Storm. 'What a shame for

Teddy,' she said sadly. 'It must be weird
living in a world of silence. Can you
use your magic to make him better?'

Storm put his head on one side. 'But
Teddy is not sick. He was born that
way. He is just different.'

Freya realized that Storm was right.
She hadn't thought of it like that. Teddy
wasn't suffering. He was a healthy
happy little dog and his silent world
was quite normal to him.

'Why don't you take Teddy back to
see the vet? She'll tell you if you're
right about him,' Gran suggested.

Freya nodded. 'Good idea, Gran.' She
turned to Isaac. 'At least you'll know that
there's a reason for the way Teddy is.'

A shadow crossed Isaac's face. 'Yeah.
But it doesn't help much, does it?'

'What do you mean?' Freya asked.

'Think about it,' Isaac said miserably. 'What's the use of taking Teddy to training classes? He's not going to be able to learn anything if he can't hear instructions. And if he won't do as he's told and keeps chewing things up, Mum and Dad will definitely re-home him!'

Freya realized that he had a point. It seemed that Isaac and Teddy were facing a whole new set of problems.

Chapter
ELEVEN

'I wonder how Isaac and Teddy are,'
Freya said to Storm a couple of
evenings later. She'd been hoping that
Isaac would phone when he'd been to
the vet, but so far she hadn't heard from
him.

Storm nodded. 'I am thinking about
them too.' He was curled up in Freya's
lap while she was reading.

When the phone rang in the hall,
Storm immediately jumped down and
ran towards it. Freya got up and
followed him.

It was Isaac. 'Hi, Freya. You were right
about Teddy,' he said at once. 'He is
deaf. The vet thinks it's a problem with
the nerves inside Teddy's ears. So he was
probably born that way.'

'Oh,' Freya said. This was one time
when she didn't feel good about being
proved right. 'I'm so sorry,' she said.

'I was too at first, but the vet's been
really good,' Isaac said, sounding quite
cheerful. 'She told me that I'll always
have to be extra careful with Teddy
near traffic and it's going to be quite
difficult to train him. But guess what,
she's got another patient who's got a

deaf dog, called Flossie and the owner
Mrs Norman has taught her to respond
to hand signals.'

'That's brilliant!' Freya enthused.

'I know. The vet phoned her up
while I was at the surgery and Mum's
taking me and Teddy over to meet
them at the weekend. Mrs Norman
only lives in the next village.'

'Oh, I'm so pleased for you,' Freya
said warmly.

Storm sat on the carpet, a curious expression on his face. Freya gave him a thumbs-up sign and Storm's tail began thumping against the carpet.

'I'm going to be at Gran's tomorrow. Why don't we meet up? You can tell me more about it,' Freya suggested. 'And I'd love to help you train Teddy . . . um . . . if you'd like me to, that is,' she said, trying to be tactful. She knew that Isaac wasn't too happy that she had managed to get Teddy to behave in the past.

'I thought you'd never ask!' She could tell that he was smiling.

Freya replaced the phone. She beamed at Storm as she told him what Isaac had said.

'I am glad for them both,' he woofed.

★

It was bright and sunny the following morning as Freya and Storm closed the door to Gran's flat and walked downstairs.

'I'm really looking forward to meeting Isaac and Teddy,' she said as they reached the bottom of the stairwell.

But Storm gave a sudden whimper of fear and shot into the side room where the wheelie bins were stored.

'Storm?' Freya heard loud barking and snarling and glimpsed some large shapes prowling about outside the glass front door. Sunlight glinted off their pale eyes and extra-long sharp teeth.

Her heart missed a beat. Storm was in terrible danger!

Freya turned and rushed after him. She reached the doorway just as a blinding flash of gold light and a shower of bright sparks lit up the wheelie-bin room.

Storm stood there, a tiny helpless puppy no longer, but a powerful young silver-grey wolf. His thick neck-ruff seemed to be gleaming with a thousand tiny yellow diamonds. Standing next to Storm was an adult she-wolf with golden eyes and a gentle expression.

A sob rose into Freya's throat as she realized that Storm was leaving. She'd hoped so much that this day wouldn't come, but she forced herself to be strong for Storm's sake.

'Shadow's dogs are almost here. Save yourself,' she urged, her voice breaking.

Storm's midnight-blue eyes softened with affection. 'Be of good heart, Freya. You have been a loyal friend,' he rumbled in a deep velvety growl.

'I'll never forget you,' Freya breathed as a tear rolled down her face.

There was a final burst of dazzling light and big golden sparks fluttered down around Freya and crackled harmlessly on to the floor.

Storm raised a huge front paw in

farewell and then he and his mother faded and were gone.

Behind Freya there was a disappointed snarling. Through the glass door, she saw three normal-looking dogs padding off awkwardly in confusion.

Sadness swept through Freya. One golden sparkle lay on the floor. She picked it up and it tickled her palm for a second before blinking out. Freya gave a bitter-sweet smile. At least she'd had a chance to say goodbye and she would always remember the wonderful adventure she had shared with her magical puppy friend.

'Take care, Storm. I hope you lead the Moon-claw pack one day,' she whispered.

Freya squared her shoulders as she went to meet Isaac and Teddy. The two of them were going to need loads of help and support and she was determined to be there for them. A warm feeling spread right through Freya as she realized that there were two new friends in her life to enjoy and she knew that Storm would always be watching over her, wherever he was.

Win a Magic Puppy goody bag!

The evil wolf Shadow has ripped out part of Storm's
letter from his mother and hidden the words so that magic puppy
Storm can't find them.

Storm needs your help!

Two words have been hidden in secret bones in *Twirling Tails*
and *School of Mischief*. Find the hidden words and put them
together to complete the message from Storm's mother.
Send it in to us and each month we will put every correct message
in a draw and pick out one lucky winner, who will receive
a Magic Puppy gift – definitely worth barking about!

Send the hidden message, your name and address on a postcard to:
Magic Puppy Competition
Puffin Books
80 Strand
London WC2R 0RL
Good luck!